In the Land of GIANTS

Christine E. Schulze

Illustrated by Karla Ortega

In loving memory of Sharon

To my "Happy Friend"
And to all my friends at Trinity Services

I took a walk in the Land of Giants. I didn't want to go, but a friend of mine suggested I visit there, just once.

When I first arrived, I didn't like it at all.
The people were big, strange, and
very different from me.

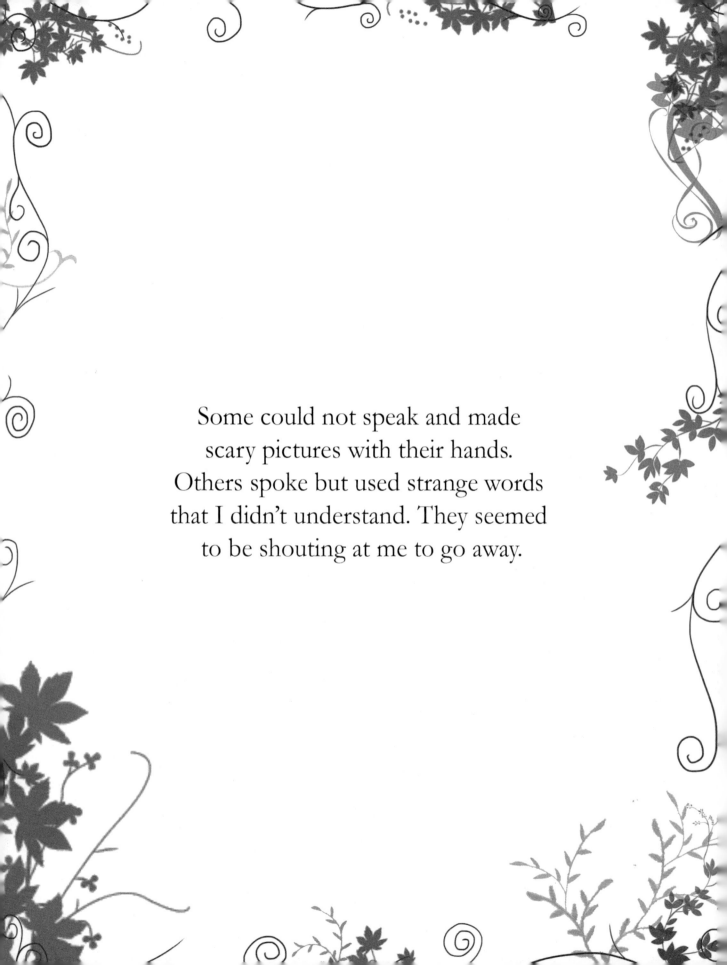

Some could not speak and made
scary pictures with their hands.
Others spoke but used strange words
that I didn't understand. They seemed
to be shouting at me to go away.

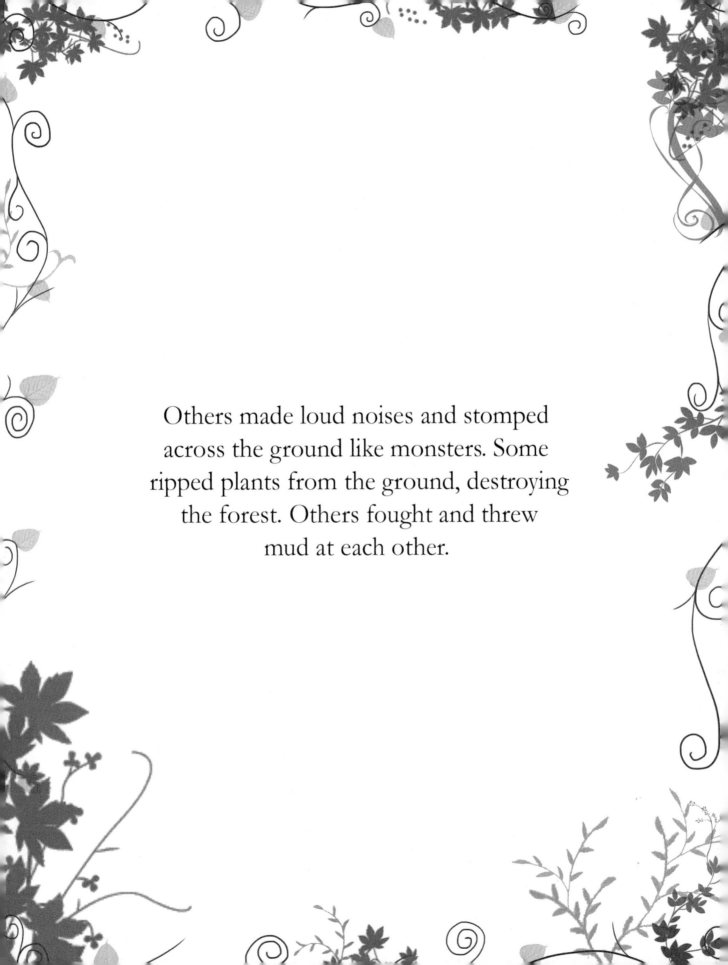

Others made loud noises and stomped across the ground like monsters. Some ripped plants from the ground, destroying the forest. Others fought and threw mud at each other.

Some couldn't see and when I bumped
into them, they yelled and waved
giant sticks at me.

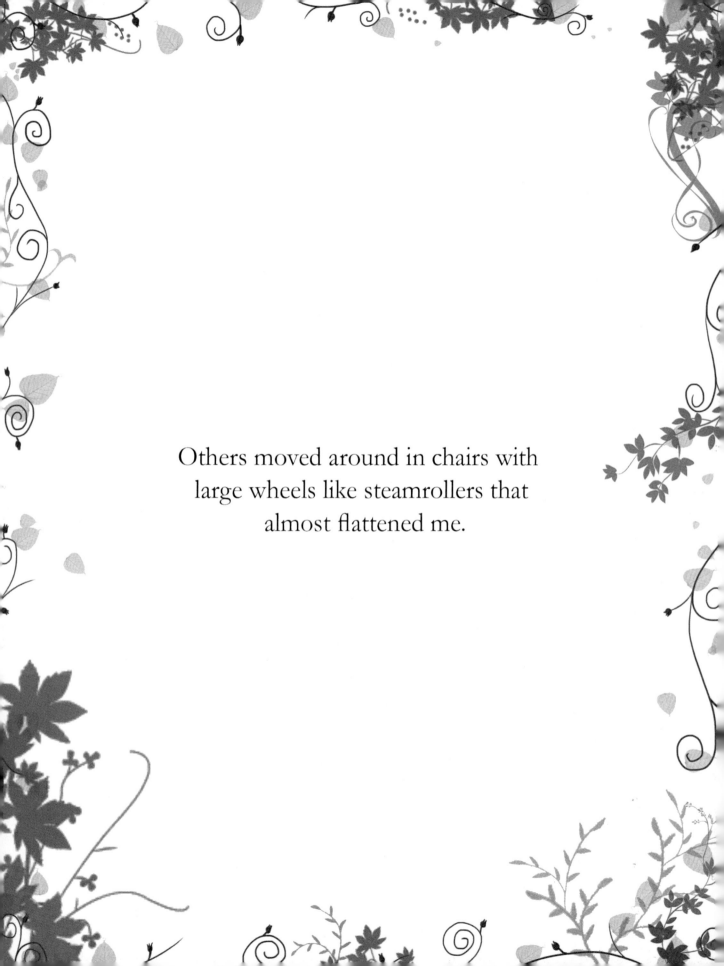

Others moved around in chairs with
large wheels like steamrollers that
almost flattened me.

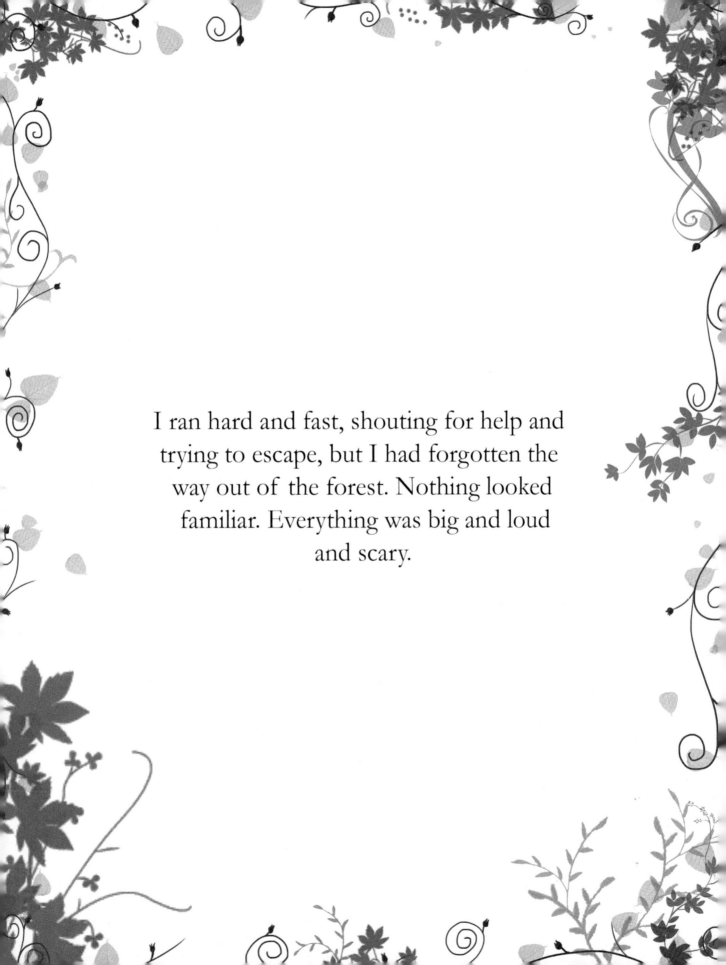

I ran hard and fast, shouting for help and trying to escape, but I had forgotten the way out of the forest. Nothing looked familiar. Everything was big and loud and scary.

I finally found a quiet place beneath
one of the lofty trees. I fell to the ground,
pulled my knees up to my chin, buried my head,
and cried. I cried harder and harder,
wishing that the Land of Giants was only a
dream from which I would soon awaken.

But no matter how many times I pinched myself, the ground still vibrated beneath me from the giants' footfalls, and in the distance, I could still hear some of them talking in their weird, unfriendly languages.

After a few moments, I heard shuffling feet come up and stop before me. I opened my eyes and gasped—a long dark shadow stretched over me. Trembling with fear, I looked up.

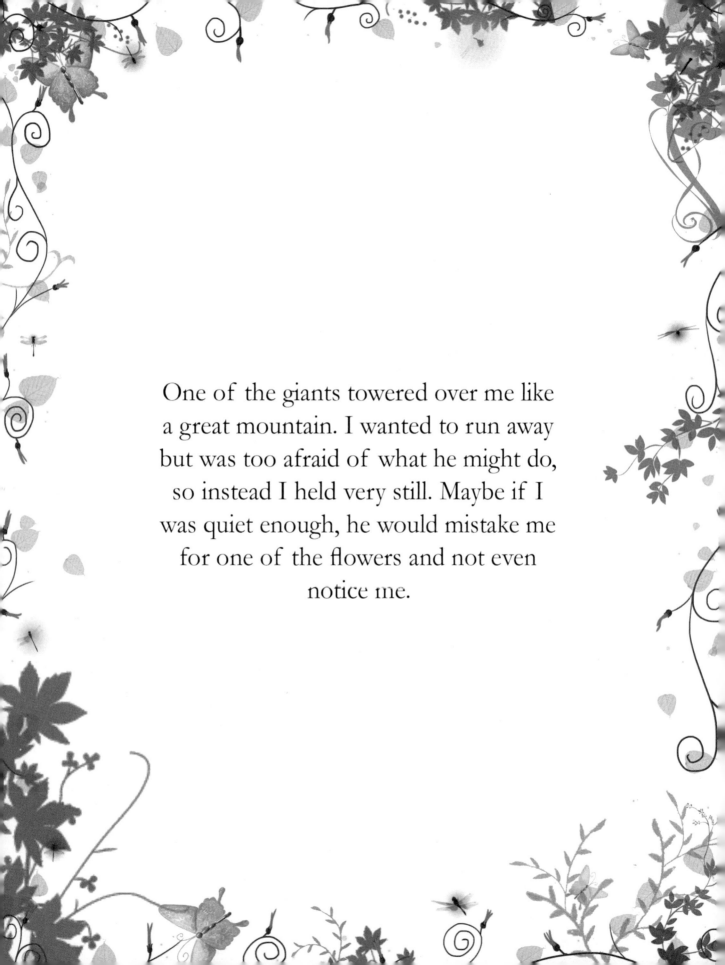

One of the giants towered over me like a great mountain. I wanted to run away but was too afraid of what he might do, so instead I held very still. Maybe if I was quiet enough, he would mistake me for one of the flowers and not even notice me.

He crouched low to the ground and stared right at me. I stared back with a shiver.

"Who are you?" he asked.

"M-my name is Matt," I said.

"What are you doing here, Matt?"

Oh, no, I thought. He knows I don't belong here. He is angry with me. Will he shout at me? Will he hit me or maybe even squish me like a tiny bug? Or maybe he will throw me in a pot of human stew and have me for supper…

"I—I'm lost," I said. "And I'm scared."

The giant furrowed his brows. He seemed to be thinking very hard. He stayed that way a long time. My heart raced as I prepared for the worst.

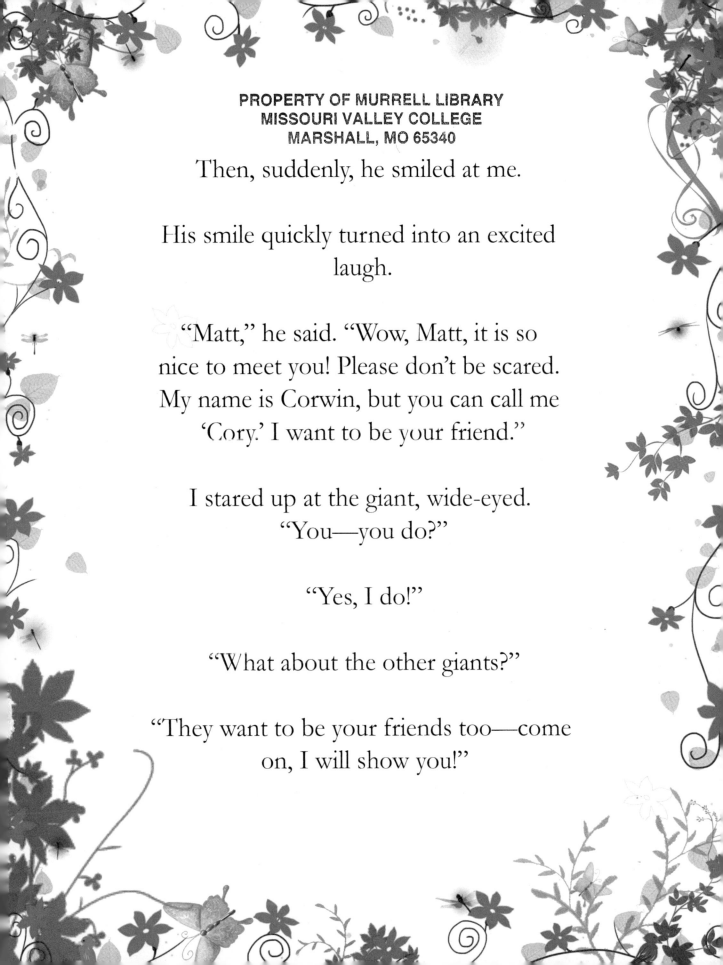

Then, suddenly, he smiled at me.

His smile quickly turned into an excited laugh.

"Matt," he said. "Wow, Matt, it is so nice to meet you! Please don't be scared. My name is Corwin, but you can call me 'Cory.' I want to be your friend."

I stared up at the giant, wide-eyed. "You—you do?"

"Yes, I do!"

"What about the other giants?"

"They want to be your friends too—come on, I will show you!"

Cory bent down and scooped me gently
in his hands.

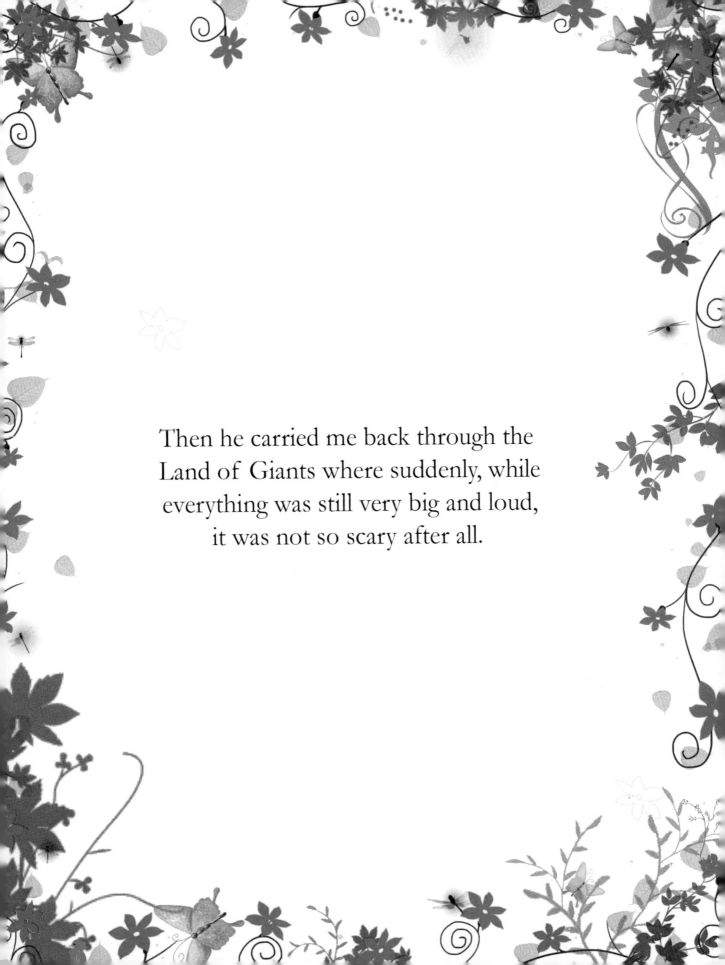

Then he carried me back through the
Land of Giants where suddenly, while
everything was still very big and loud,
it was not so scary after all.

Some of the giants used their hand-pictures
to sing beautiful songs. Others sang with
their voices. They seemed to love Christmas
songs, just like me, and I joined in.
Cory sang too.

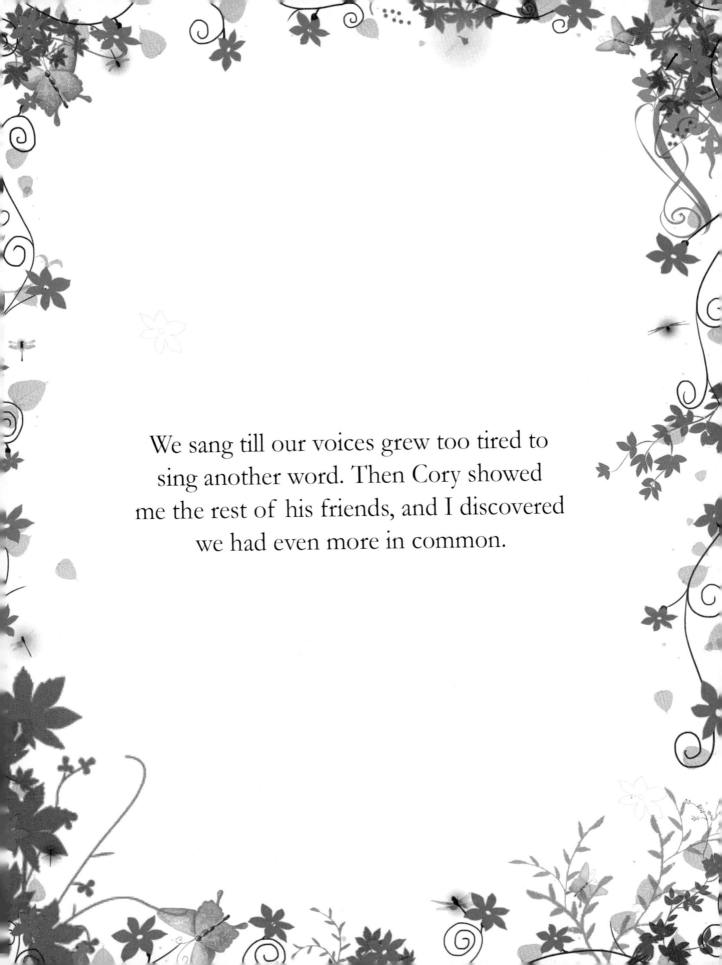

We sang till our voices grew too tired to
sing another word. Then Cory showed
me the rest of his friends, and I discovered
we had even more in common.

They didn't destroy the forest or throw mud at each other. Instead, they harvested all kinds of vegetables from their gardens and picked fruit from the trees. One of them offered me and Cory some strawberries. We thanked her and gladly devoured them.

Some of Cory's other friends painted bright, colorful decorations to hang in the trees. We asked if we could help, and they answered with an excited, "Yes!" I painted a large picture of a super hero, looking at Cory's shirt as a guide.

"I love your super hero shirt," I told him.
"It's just like mine!"

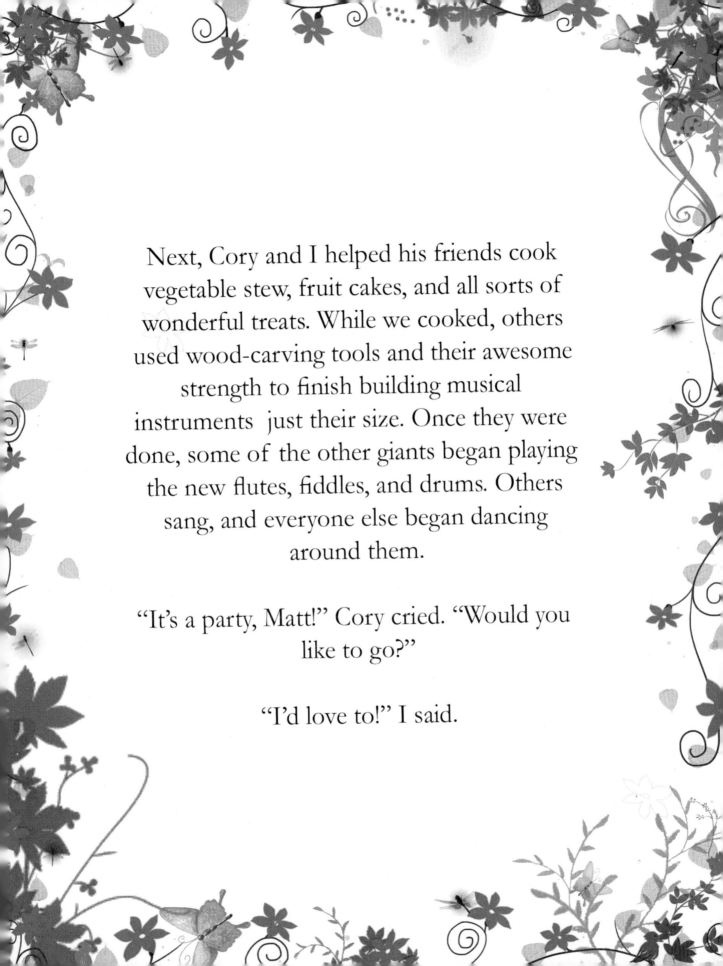

Next, Cory and I helped his friends cook vegetable stew, fruit cakes, and all sorts of wonderful treats. While we cooked, others used wood-carving tools and their awesome strength to finish building musical instruments just their size. Once they were done, some of the other giants began playing the new flutes, fiddles, and drums. Others sang, and everyone else began dancing around them.

"It's a party, Matt!" Cory cried. "Would you like to go?"

"I'd love to!" I said.

Cory's friends fast became mine. We danced and sang and ate good food until it was so late that the stars glowed like millions of night-lights above, until I couldn't stop yawning and my eyes would hardly stay open.

Then Cory scooped me up in his gentle hands again and said, "I think it is bedtime, Matt. I will take you home."

I nodded, yawned again, and let him carry me.

Before I knew it, Cory was reaching his giant hands through the open window of my bedroom and setting me carefully on my bed. I drew my blanket up around my shoulders and gazed up at him with a smile.

"Neat poster!" Cory said. "It has super heroes on it just like our shirts."

"Yeah, it does," I said with a sleepy yawn and smile. "Thanks for inviting me to the party, but I think I'd better get to sleep."

"Okay, Matt," Cory said. With a wave, he added, "Please come back to visit us sometime."

"Oh, I will," I said, waving back. "I definitely will. Good night!"

"Good night!"

Cory turned away from my window, and I snuggled deep beneath my covers. As Cory walked away, I could hear his giant footsteps and feel my whole house shake a little. I smiled, for the shaking and the noise no longer frightened me. They no longer made me think of big, scary monsters. They made me think of my new friends. How silly I had been to be scared before.

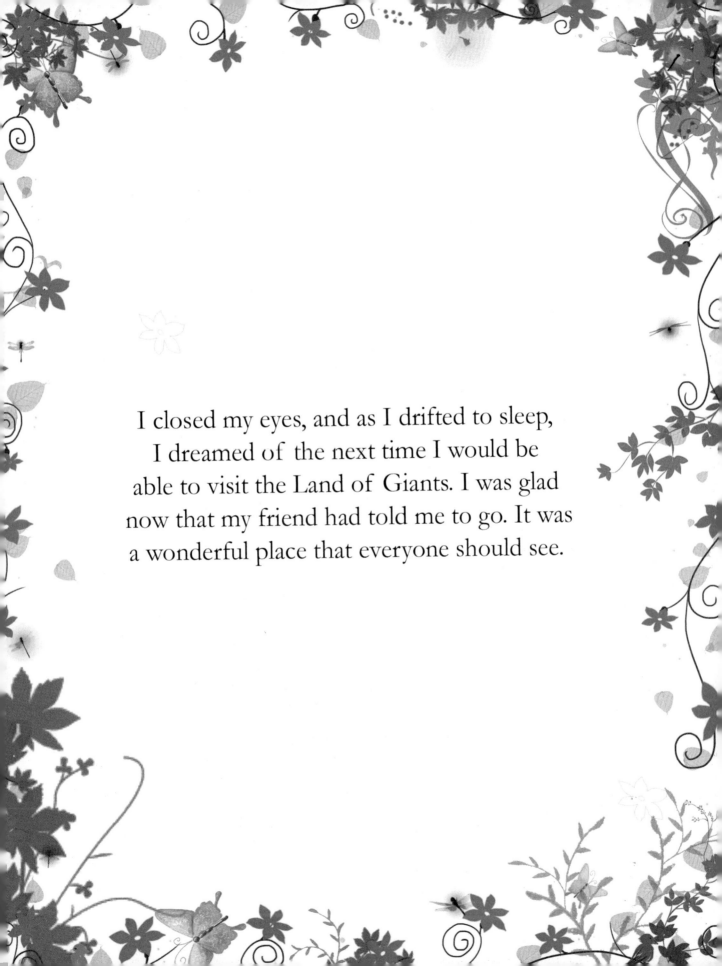

I closed my eyes, and as I drifted to sleep,
I dreamed of the next time I would be
able to visit the Land of Giants. I was glad
now that my friend had told me to go. It was
a wonderful place that everyone should see.

Next time, I think I'll even invite a new friend to come with me.

Author's Note

Hi, and thanks so much for joining Matt, Cory, and the rest of the Giants on their adventure!

Ever since I was a young writer, I have been keenly aware of the need for more diversity in fantasy literature—young adult, children's, or otherwise—and have strived to implement this in my own books. I started out trying to include various races so that people of color could be represented more as main characters.

However, more recently, an even greater need has been brought to light, and with it, an even greater passion.

A little over a year ago, I began working for an organization that offers day programs and residential services to adults with disabilities. At first, I was uncertain about the job because I had never worked with people with disabilities. But I had taught daycare and preschool for a number of years and hoped that my background and education in teaching would aid me.

After being on the job for a week, I was sent to work at a site we affectionately call "The Farm." I quickly fell in love and have been in love ever since. The Farm is a place brimming with constant life and activity. There's never a dull moment, and every day we get to teach the clients—and often ourselves—many things like culinary, gardening, art, math, social skills, and life skills. Community outings are always a treat. Someone even donated a piano this past year; since then, gathering together to sing songs has become one of everyone's favorite pastimes.

People with disabilities are amazing people with talents, goals, and dreams, just like everyone else. So, one of my newest personal goals is to include more main characters with disabilities in my books. People in this group are rarely represented in fantastical fiction, and I want to do my part to show that they can be heroes too!

In addition to *In the Land of Giants*, I am simultaneously releasing *The Amazing K*, a zany, outer space fantasy adventure for young readers that features characters who fly around in a rocket-propelled wheelchair, use sign-language, and even rock a mechanical arm that shoots zappy lasers! Such characters and stories prove that it's cool to be different, and with enough imagination, disabilities can never hold you back.

I am also donating twenty-five percent of all royalties from my current publications to ALFA, a charity that funds many of the programs that service our adults with disabilities locally, such as providing volunteers and supplies for culinary, gardening, art, and more. Thus, by owning this book, you're not only sharing in an adventure about folks with disabilities—you're also giving back to the ones who helped inspire it!

Thanks again for joining me on this adventure. I hope you will join me for many more!

~ Christine E. Schulze

Dear Readers,

I would like to hear from you—no, I really, really would!

One of my favorite things about being an author is getting the opportunity to meet, speak with, and get to know my readers on a more personal level. What truly excites me about being an author today is that there are a variety of ways authors and readers can easily connect with one another.

If you enjoyed the story you just read—or even if you didn't—feel free to leave an honest review at any of these websites: Goodreads, Barnes and Noble, and/or Amazon. Hopping online to see what my readers have to say about my books really motivates me as an author. Whether you absolutely loved the story, have constructive criticism to give, or simply want to share your thoughts with friends and family about the new author you've just discovered, any feedback is appreciated and helps me out!

If you have any questions for me or just want to say "hello," you can find me on Facebook or Goodreads. Also, at my website: http://christineschulze.com

Or, if you're old fashioned like me and enjoy writing letters, you can reach me at the following:

Email: ChristineESchulze@gmail.com

Snail Mail: Christine E. Schulze
             18 Archview Drive
             Belleville, IL 62221

Thanks so much for your support! I look forward to hearing from you and hope we can share in many more adventures together.

~ Christine E. Schulze

The Amielian Legacy

The Amielian Legacy is a vast fantasy comprised of both stand-alone books and series for ages ranging from children to young adult. *The Amielian Legacy* creates a fantastical history for North America in much the same way that Tolkien's Middle Earth created a mythology for Europe. While it's not necessary to read any particular book or series to read the others, they do ultimately weave together to create a single overarching mythology.

Stand-Alone Books

Bloodmaiden (Second Edition)
Lily in the Snow (Second Edition)
Larimar: Gem of the Sea
Dream Catcher, Heart Listener
Beyond the Veil
Follow Me
Tears of a Vampire Prince
The Chronicles of the Mira
The Crystal Rings
Song Quest
Black Lace/Dark Embrace
The Adventures of William the Brownie
In the Land of Giants
The Amazing K
The Pirates of Meleeon
The Last Star (No release date yet)
Carousel in the Clouds (No release date yet)

The Amielian Legacy (*cont.*)

Series

The Stregoni Sequence
Golden Healer, Dark Enchantress
Memory Charmer
Wish Granter

A Shadow Beyond Time (with co-author Kira Lerner)
The Undying Portal (No release date yet)
The Awakening Army (No release date yet)
The Mourning Birds (No release date yet)
The Darkling Shadow (No release date yet)
The Bleeding Veil (No release date yet)

The Gailean Quartet (Second Editions; first release 2016)

The Legends of Surprisers
The Legends of Surprisers, Book I (No release date yet)
The Legends of Surprisers, Book II (No release date yet)
The Legends of Surprisers, Book III: The Vision (No release date yet)

D.N.A. Sequence (No release date yet)

Made in the USA
Columbia, SC
06 May 2019